P9-APR-063

Girls Play to Win

TRACK & FIELD

by Chrös McDougall

Content Consultant
Elliot Denman
U.S. Olympic Racewalker

Norwood House Press
CHICAGO, ILLINOIS

Norwood House Press
P.O. Box 316598
Chicago, Illinois 60631

For information regarding Norwood House Press, please visit our website at
www.norwoodhousepress.com or call 866-565-2900.

Photo Credits: Darko Bandic/AP Images, cover; Anja Niedringhaus/AP Images, 4;
Shutterstock Images, 7; Bigstock, 8, 11, 52, 55; Tom Oliveira/Bigstock, 9; Sportgraphic/
Shutterstock Images, 12, 50; Jim Parkin/Shutterstock Images, 14; Tolga Bayraktar/
iStockphoto, 18; Vassar College, Archives & Special Collections, 21; Library of
Congress, 22, 24, 26, 29, 30; AP Images, 31, 32, 36; RW/AP Images, 34; Ragne Kabanova/
Bigstock, 39; Lennox McLendon/AP Images, 40, 41; Al Behrman/AP Images, 45; Pete
Nielsen/Shutterstock Images, 48; Lee Jin-man/AP Images, 57; Chrös McDougall, 64
(top); Elliot Denman, 64 (bottom)

Editor: Holly Saari
Series Design and Cover Production: Christa Schneider
Interior Production: Craig Hinton
Project Management: Red Line Editorial

Library of Congress Cataloging-in-Publication Data

McDougall, Chrös.
Girls play to win track & field / by Chrös McDougall.
   p. cm. -- (Girls play to win)
Includes bibliographical references and index.
Summary: "Covers the history, rules, fundamentals, and significant
personalities of the sport of women's track and field. Topics include:
techniques, strategies, competitive events, and equipment. Glossary,
Additional Resources and Index included"--Provided by publisher.
ISBN-13: 978-1-59953-467-1 (library edition : alk. paper)
ISBN-10: 1-59953-467-3 (library edition : alk. paper)
1. Track and field for women--Juvenile literature. I. Title.
GV1060.8.M44 2011
796.42082--dc22
                              2011011053

Manufactured in the United States of America in North Mankato, Minnesota.
177N—072011

Girls Play to Win

TRACK & FIELD

Table of Contents

Words in **bold type** are defined in the glossary.

▲ Lolo Jones (right) competing in the
100-meter hurdles in the 2008 Olympic Games

Beijing 2008 ⚪⚪⚪

CHAPTER 1

TRACK-AND-FIELD
BASICS

More than 90,000 people at the Bird's Nest stadium in Beijing, China, turned their attention to the start of the 100-meter **hurdles**. In lane four, Lolo Jones was the favorite to win the Olympic gold medal.

The hurdler from Des Moines, Iowa, had come a long way to get there. She grew up poor and was even homeless for a time. But Jones focused her efforts on hurdling. That took her to Louisiana State University, where she starred on the track and got a college degree. Now, at the 2008 Olympic Games, it was her time to shine.

The gun sounded to start the race. By the eighth of 10 hurdles, Jones was pulling away. And then it happened. Jones clipped the ninth hurdle. She stayed on her feet but her speed was gone. The pre-race favorite finished seventh and fell to the ground in shock.

Jones was shaken, but she never gave up. Not even after an injury-filled 2009 season. She finally got redemption in 2010. At the 2010 World Indoor Championships, Jones defended her world title in the 60-meter hurdles with a time of 7.72 seconds. With hard work and dedication, Jones had climbed back to the top. Throughout its history and development, women's track and field has had many athletes just like Jones who never gave up.

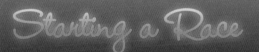

Starting a Race

When getting ready to start a race, the starter first says, "On your marks." This is when you step forward and do one last stretch or movement to loosen up. When the judge says, "set," you must get behind the starting line and get in position to start. When the starting gun fires, go!

GETTING STARTED

Track and field, also known as athletics, consists of a series of tests, or events, in running, racewalking, jumping, and throwing. The intent is to determine who can do each event the fastest, highest, or farthest. The sport is divided into track events and field events. Many athletes, especially beginners, compete in multiple events. A competition in track and field is called a **meet**.

TRACK

Track events involve racing on a running track. A standard outdoor track is 400 meters long. Indoor tracks are generally 200 meters long.

World Champions

The Olympic Games have always been the biggest competition in track and field. The Games only take place every four years, though, and the sport runs continuously. In order to determine the world's best during non-Olympic years, the outdoor World Championships were created in 1983. The World Indoor Championships began in 1985. Today, each event takes place every two years, with World Championships taking place every odd year and World Indoor Championships taking place every even year.

▲ *Tracks are oval shaped and usually include a field inside the lanes.*

SPRINTS

The shortest and fastest races in a meet are the sprints. The most common sprint events in outdoor meets are the 100-, 200-, and 400-meter dashes. Indoor meets occasionally have different distances, such as the 60-meter dash. In such short races, margins of victory are often very small. That means sprinters must have good running form in order to maximize their speed.

With such short distances, successful starting is very important. Most sprinters begin a race in **starting blocks**. The blocks give the runner something to push off. Some people call this "exploding" out of the blocks. The sprinters then accelerate until they reach their full speed. The first person whose **torso** crosses the finish line wins.

▲ *Sprinters explode out of the starting blocks.*

Sprint events are also competed in as relays. The most common are the 4x100-, 4x200-, and 4x400-meter relays. In these, each runner on a team runs the same distance. There are **medley** relays as well. These are relays in which a team works together to run the total distance. In a medley, one runner on a team may run a different distance than another. A relay begins with a start out of the blocks like individual sprint races. When one teammate has completed her part of the race, she hands a baton to the next teammate. The handoff occurs at a run. Elite runners are trained to make the handoffs without looking.

Lanes on an outdoor track

TRACK-AND-FIELD LINGO

anchor: *The final runner on a relay team.*

clear: *Successfully leaping over a hurdle or the bar in high jump or pole vault. You can hit the bar, but as long as it stays up you have cleared it.*

false start: *When a runner begins before the starting gun fires. Depending on the competition, one or two false starts result in disqualification.*

foul: *Either a violation of regulations during a field event or an action against another runner in a race deemed to have hindered that runner's race.*

lanes: *Parallel courses on a track that runners must stay in for some or all of a race. Tracks usually have eight or nine lanes.*

lap: *One full journey around the track or course.*

personal best: *Your best result in a given event. Many people simply say "PB."*

The track-and-field community often uses metric measurements. Nonmetric races such as the 100-yard dash and the 220-yard dash, which had once been common in the United States, are rare today. However, the metric measurements are often close to their standard counterparts and are sometimes known as such. For example, the 1,600-meter run is very close to a mile, so it is often referred to as the "metric mile." The 800-meter run is similar to a half-mile race. In kilometers, five equal 3.1 miles and 10 equal 6.2 miles.

HURDLES

In sprint races called hurdles, obstacles are set up on the track. The goal is to clear the obstacles, or hurdles, without losing speed. Just clipping a hurdle can slow a runner down, as Lolo Jones's story shows. The best hurdlers can clear the hurdles very closely without actually touching them.

Women compete in the 100-meter hurdles. At the highest levels, they also compete in the 400-meter hurdles. The hurdles in the 100 are higher than those in the 400. At youth levels, girls often compete in 300-meter **intermediate** hurdles.

MIDDLE AND LONG DISTANCE

The 800-, 1,500-, and 1,600-meter runs are middle-distance races. These events require more strategy than sprints because runners have to conserve energy. These athletes have a mix of a sprinter's speed and a distance-runner's **stamina**. Because of that, some people believe middle-distance events are the most challenging track events.

Long-distance events are the longest running events on the track. On the elite level, they include events such as the 3,000-, 5,000-, and 10,000-meter runs. The longest race in high school meets is usually either 3,000 or 3,200 meters. Distance runners need to have superb stamina. The races involve many **laps** around the track and take several minutes to complete. As such, **pacing** is very important. Starting too fast can burn a runner out by the end. Starting too slow can let her fall so far behind she cannot catch up toward the

Cross-country is often run on grass courses.

CROSS-COUNTRY & ROAD RUNNING

*Long-distance races that take place off a track are a good way for middle- and long-distance runners to **cross train**. Cross-country racing is a common format. In cross-country, athletes run distances usually starting around 4,000 meters or longer on natural terrain. Outside cross-country, road races are also very popular on both a recreational and an elite level. These are often races that take place on city streets or in parks. They run from one mile to 5,000 meters to marathons (26.2 miles).*

▲ *It's important for middle- and long-distance runners not to fall too far behind the group at any point during the race.*

end. A strong kick, or burst of speed at the end of the race, is considered a very important ability.

Middle- and long-distance runners usually start from a standing position. Unlike sprints and hurdles, these athletes are allowed to leave their lanes at a designated mark beyond the start. For maximum efficiency, the runners try to stay as close to the inside of the track as possible.

FIELD

Field events involve some form of jumping or throwing. The venue for each field event is slightly different.

THROWS

There are five throwing events. Discus, javelin, and hammer throw take place in outdoor venues. Shot put takes place in outdoor and indoor competitions. Weight throw usually takes place only indoors. The goal of each event is to throw the object the farthest. The weight of each object depends on the level of competition.

Shot put, discus, hammer throw, and weight throw are similar. They involve an athlete standing in a small circle, called the **ring**, and throwing the object into a cone-shaped field of play. Stepping out of the circle or throwing outside the field of play results in a **foul**. Depending on the competition, athletes usually have three or six throws.

A shot put is a heavy metal ball. The athlete begins with the shot put near her shoulder and hurls it into the field of play. In the discus and hammer and weight throws, the athlete flings the object into the field of play from her side. A discus is a disc-shaped weight. A hammer is a heavy metal ball that has a steel wire connecting it to a handle. The weight is a heavy object with a handle. In each of these four events, elite throwers spin before letting go of the respective objects to give them more force. The javelin throw differs from the other throwing events.

▲ *Discus is thrown from the ring, and a net is behind it for safety, in case the discus is released too soon in the athlete's spin.*

In this event, the athlete runs down a runway and then throws a long spear.

Throwing requires more than strength to be successful. Top throwers are also quick, agile, and coordinated. Good technique can also separate good throwers from the best.

JUMPS

There are two kinds of jumping events. One type is for distance. The other type is for height. The long jump and triple jump measure distance. High jump and pole vault measure height.

Long jump and triple jump are very similar. In both, the athletes sprint down a runway and then leap with one foot off a takeoff **board**. They land in a sandpit. The final distance is measured from the takeoff board to the nearest mark in the sand. Athletes generally have three or six jumps per competition. If the foot steps beyond the takeoff board, the jump is a foul. Athletes are able to mark an ideal starting point on the runway so they can have a fair takeoff right as they reach full speed.

In long jump, the athlete leaps once before landing in the sand. In triple jump, after the initial leap, the athlete hops a second time off her original takeoff foot and a third time on the opposite foot before landing in the sandpit. The moves are known as hop, step, and jump.

In high jump, athletes must clear a bar after jumping off one foot. Most high jumpers begin off to one side. They take a running start and then leap backwards over the bar. The athlete continues until she fails three consecutive attempts.

Pole vault is similar to high jump in that the athlete attempts to clear a bar. However, the heights in pole vault are much higher. The athletes use a long, flexible pole to propel themselves high into the air. The event begins on a long runway. Once the athlete reaches the end, she plants the pole into the vault box and uses her **momentum** to rise into the air with her pole and, hopefully, clear the bar feet first. As in high jump, the pole-vaulter can continue until she has three consecutive misses. The event requires all-around athleticism, and it can be dangerous without proper instruction.

MULTI-EVENTS

In higher levels of track and field, athletes can compete in multi-event competitions such as the heptathlon. The heptathlon combines seven track-and-field events over a span of two days. Three are running events, two are jumping, and two are throwing. It is designed to determine the top overall athlete by testing a wide range of skills.

Racewalking

Track events do not only involve running. In fact, in the event of racewalking, running disqualifies an athlete. In racewalking, a competitor must always have one foot on the ground. The front leg must also straighten during each step. A racewalker who crosses the boundary from walking to running receives a foul. Too many fouls during a race result in disqualification. Two racewalking events are in the Olympic Games. The 20-kilometer race, which both men and women compete in, and the 50-kilometer race, which only men compete in.

▲ *Discus was a throwing event in the ancient Olympic Games.*

CHAPTER 2

ANCIENT
ORIGINS

The earliest known athletics took place in Egypt around 3500 BCE. Hundreds of years later, track-and-field events were featured at the ancient Olympic Games in Olympia, Greece, in 776 BCE. These Games featured running, jumping, and throwing events, as well as non-track-and-field sports. However, only Greek men who were not slaves could compete. Married women could not even attend.

Instead, women competed in a separate event called the Heraia. It took place every four years at the stadium in Olympia. However, the only event was an approximately 160-meter footrace. The women split into three different groups depending on their age. The winners received a crown made of an olive wreath.

TRACK AND FIELD

Smaller-scale athletics competitions continued throughout Europe after the ancient Olympic Games ended around the year 400. It was in the British Isles, however, where modern track and field was invented. Athletics meets had been held in Britain since the 12th century.

Cross-Country

Like modern track and field, cross-country also originated in the United Kingdom during the 19th century. It began with one team dropping paper along a random route and a second team following that paper trail. The sport evolved into what we know it as today, and it began spreading to other countries later in the century. Men's cross-country was at the 1912, 1920, and 1924 Olympic Games. The first international women's cross-country race took place in 1931 in France. However, women's cross-country did not have a world championship event until 1967.

When schools and universities there began to standardize the rules during the 1800s, official track and field was created. Track and field began to spread around the world. However, opportunities for women to compete were still very slim. Thanks to a small college in New York, that would soon begin to change.

VASSAR FIELD DAY

On November 9, 1895, Vassar College in Poughkeepsie, New York, did something that had never happened before: It held a women's track-and-field meet. Twenty-two female students came to the oval field to compete. Nearly 400 more people watched. Only one of them, the meet referee, was a man. Many people did not approve of

Women's World Games

The Women's World Games was held three more times following its successful debut in 1922. The Women's World Games even continued in 1930 and 1934, after women's track and field was accepted into the Olympic Games. The Women's World Games continued because Alice Milliat and other organizers were unsatisfied with the amount of women's events at the Olympic Games. The final Women's World Games took place in 1934 in London, England. Athletes from 19 countries competed in 12 events. Women only competed in six events at the 1932 Olympic Games.

▲ *Vassar Field Day, 1899. Women competed in skirts during the events.*

women taking part in strenuous and competitive activity at the time, so the school did its best to keep men and reporters out.

Field Day included five track-and-field events: 100-yard dash, 120-yard hurdles, 220-yard dash, high jump, and long jump. The college added five more events the next year. They were fence vault, standing broad jump, throwing the basketball, throwing the baseball, and 300-yard relay. As Vassar Field Day continued throughout the years, women at other universities became eager to test themselves. Similar women's track-and-field meets popped up around the country.

▲ *Women competing in a hurdle race between 1920 and 1930*

GETTING TO THE GAMES

After approximately 1,500 years, the Olympic Games returned in 1896 as a multisport, international event. Women were first allowed to compete in the second modern Games in 1900, but only in tennis, golf, and croquet. More women's sports were added over the next several Games. Yet by 1920, women were still not allowed to compete in Olympic track and field.

A French woman named Alice Milliat worked hard to change that. She first led a movement to get the women's sport added to the 1920 Games. But the International Olympic Committee (IOC) deemed the sport inappropriate for women. Not one to get discouraged, Milliat formed the Fédération Sportive Féminine Internationale (FSFI). The group gave women an opportunity to compete internationally.

In 1922, Milliat and the FSFI took things a step further when they hosted the Women's World Games in Paris, France. More than 20,000 fans showed up to watch women compete in 11 track-and-field events. Despite the success, the IOC still did not budge. It kept women out of track-and-field events at the 1924 Olympic Games. However, the International Amateur Athletic Federation (IAAF) decided to allow women to join that year. The IAAF is the world governing body for track and field. At the next vote, the IOC finally added women's track-and-field events to the 1928 Olympic Games in Amsterdam, Netherlands.

Alice Milliat

Alice Milliat was once a star rower in her native France. She was also one of the leaders pushing to get women's track and field into the Olympic Games. When that continued to be rejected, she headed up the first international women's track meet in 1921. The momentum following that event's success led her to found the FSFI later that year and the Women's World Games in 1922. Behind Milliat's leadership, women's track and field became organized and standardized and was finally accepted into the Olympic Games.

▲ *A woman competes in the high jump at the 1928 Games.*

Margaret Jenkins

When Margaret Jenkins began track and field during the early 1920s, most women still wore pants while competing. In search of more flexibility, Jenkins switched to shorts. Before long, shorts became the norm. Jenkins had an impact on more than just wardrobes, though. The 5-foot-6 (1.7 m), 142-pound (64.4-kg) Jenkins was perhaps the United States' first great thrower. She won more than 100 medals while competing in javelin, shot put, discus, and other throwing events. Her best event was the javelin, in which she set two world records.

The first Olympic women's track-and-field meet had only five events. They were the 100- and 800-meter races, high jump, discus, and 4x100 relay. Many men were still unsure about women competing in track and field. The IOC would even try to remove women's track and field from the 1932 Olympics. But women were there to stay.

▲ *Mildred "Babe" Didrikson (right) runs the 80-meter hurdles at the 1932 Olympics.*

CHAPTER 3

THE BABE LEADS

Competitive sports for women were largely shunned through the 1920s and 1930s. That did not stop Mildred "Babe" Didrikson. Born in 1911 in Port Arthur, Texas, Didrikson said that from a young age, "My goal was to be the greatest athlete that ever lived." With stellar careers in track and field, golf, basketball, and many other sports, she may just have succeeded.

Didrikson's outspoken nature and muscular appearance went against what many believed a woman should be during her era. She never let that hold her back, though. Growing up the sixth of seven children in a working-class family, Didrikson was drawn to sports from an early age. She excelled at just about any sport she tried, including track and field, which she took up in 1930.

The 5-foot-5 (1.7-m), 105-pound (47.6-kg) athlete started strong by setting a new javelin world record in 1930. In 1932, Didrikson competed in eight events at the national championships. She won and set world records in the javelin, 80-meter hurdles, high jump, shot put, and baseball throw. She tied for first place in high jump and finished fourth in discus. She also ran the 100-meter dash.

Didrikson qualified to compete in five events at the 1932 Olympic Games, which were in Los Angeles,

Teams

Since women's track and field was largely shunned in the United States during the early part of the 20th century, few schools and universities had programs. Many young athletes, such as Babe Didrikson, were able to compete in meets thanks to companies that sponsored teams. Didrikson, for example, competed for the Employers Casualty Company, which sold insurance.

Scoring

Track meets are often scored as team events. Although the numbers differ by meet, the top finisher in each event earns the maximum points and each additional finisher earns slightly fewer. The team with the most points at the end wins the meet.

Babe Didrikson was the only competitor for her team, Employers Casualty Company, at the 1932 national championships. Even so, her 30 points were enough to win the team competition. The second-place team had 22 athletes and finished with 22 points.

California. However, rules at the time stated she could only compete in three. Didrikson won gold medals in javelin (43.68 meters/143 feet 4 inches) and the 80-meter hurdles (11.7 seconds). Although she and fellow U.S. competitor Jean Shiley each set a new world record in high jump (1.6 meters/5 feet 3 inches), Shiley was awarded the gold medal. The judges controversially ruled that Didrikson's deciding jump used an illegal technique, even though she had been using it throughout the competition. Nevertheless, the "Texas Tornado," as Didrikson was also known, became the first superstar in women's track and field. For her efforts in track and field and other sports, Didrikson was also voted the greatest female athlete of the first half of the 20th century by the Associated Press.

▲ *Didrikson won gold in javelin in 1932.*

Fanny Blankers-Koen won the 200 at the 1946 Olympic Games.

QUEEN OF THE TRACK

Fanny Blankers-Koen followed Babe Didrikson as track and field's biggest star. Blankers-Koen competed in the 1936, 1948, and 1952 Olympic Games. All four of her gold medals came at the 1948 Games. That matched American male Jesse Owens's record haul of four track-and-field gold medals set at the 1936 Games. Blankers-Koen was 30 years old and a mother of two children when she did it. During her career Blankers-Koen set 20 world records. The IAAF later named her the top female athlete of the century.

TUSKEGEE AND TENNESSEE STATE

The intensity of the sport continued to turn some people off. Few U.S. schools and universities supported the sport from the 1930s through the 1950s. Two traditionally African-American universities were the exception.

Tuskegee Institute in Alabama and Tennessee State University (TSU) led women's track-and-field teams during that era. Many of the U.S. Olympians came from these schools. One of them was Alice Coachman. She was a star high jumper at Tuskegee, winning 10 straight national outdoor titles. At the 1948 Olympic Games, she became the first African American to win a gold medal. She won the high jump with a leap of 1.68 meters (5 feet 6 1/8 inches).

▲ *Alice Coachman (center) wins the 100-meter dash at a meet in 1946.*

During a time of racial discrimination in the country, the athletes proved African Americans were equal to whites. They still faced discrimination in the United States, but the Tuskegee and TSU track-and-field programs continued on strong. And the best was yet to come.

Alice Coachman

In 1948, Alice Coachman became the first African American to win an Olympic gold medal when she won the high jump with an Olympic-record leap of 1.68 meters (5 feet 6 1/8 inches). Coachman was the dominant U.S. high jumper during the 1940s. She was also a star sprinter and basketball player at Tuskegee Institute and later Albany State College.

▲ *Wilma Rudolph explodes from the blocks during a heat of the 200-meter dash at the 1960 Games.*

CHAPTER 4

DEFYING THE ODDS

The odds were stacked against Wilma Rudolph from the start. She was born in 1940 as the twentieth of 22 children in a poor African-American family from segregated Tennessee. When Rudolph was four, she was diagnosed with polio, which partly paralyzed her left leg. Doctors said she might never walk normally again.

Rudolph was not one to give up, though. She began treatment on her legs. By age 10, she was walking without a brace. At 12, she said, "I was challenging every boy in our neighborhood at running, jumping, everything." At age 14, she began working out as a sprinter at TSU's campus. Two years later, she was on the other side of the world in Melbourne, Australia, to compete at the 1956 Olympic Games. The 16-year-old did not make the finals in the 200-meter dash, but she came home with a bronze medal in the 4x100 relay. The future looked bright for Rudolph.

By 1960, the 20-year-old Rudolph was atop the world of women's track and field. The Games that year were in Rome, Italy. There, Rudolph tied the world record in the 100-meter dash (11.3 seconds) and broke an Olympic record in the 200-meter dash (23.2 seconds). She won gold medals in both events. Then, running the anchor leg of the 4x100 relay, Rudolph overcame a bobbled handoff to run down a West German runner and win another gold. That made her the first U.S. woman to win three gold medals on the track in one Olympic Games. Rudolph retired from track two years later, but her impact on the sport was great.

CHANGES IN TRACK

Even after Rudolph took the nation by storm with her success in the 1960 Olympics, women's track and field

Wyomia Tyus (left) running in the 4x100 relay at the 1968 Olympic Games

THE TIGERBELLES

From 1950 to 1994, 40 TSU Tigerbelles competed in the Olympic Games—35 of them for the United States. Those athletes won a combined 13 gold medals, six silver medals, and four bronze medals. All but one of those Olympians earned her college degree.

Some Tigerbelles stood above the rest, including Wilma Rudolph. At the 1968 Games, Wyomia Tyus became the first athlete to win back-to-back gold medals in the 100 with a world-record 11.08-second run. She also added a gold medal in the 4x100 relay in 1968. That same year, Madeline Manning became the first—and through 2008 the only—U.S. woman to win an Olympic gold medal in the 800. She set an Olympic record in the process at 2:00.09, or two minutes and nine-tenths of a second. Willye B. White only spent a short time at TSU, but she became the first American to compete in five Olympic Games, from 1956 through 1972. She earned two silver medals—one in long jump and one in the 4x100 relay—and was the top U.S. long jumper for much of that time.

was still shunned by many in the United States and other parts of the world. The years around Rudolph's success did see some major growth in the sport, though. Several events were added and changed in the Olympic program over the next several years:

- **1948:** The women's 200-meter dash, shot put, and long jump were added.

- **1960:** Women were allowed to compete in the 800-meter race.

- **1964:** The 400-meter dash and the pentathlon—a competition of five events—debuted.

- **1972:** After 40 years of the 80-meter hurdles, the event was upgraded to the 100-meter hurdles. This Olympics also recognized a growing trend by adding the 1,500-meter run.

SOVIET UNION STARS

Around the mid-1900s, many of the top women's track-and-field athletes came from the Eastern Bloc countries and the former Soviet Union. Romania's Iolanda Balas set 14 world records and won two Olympic gold medals in the high jump during the 1950s and 1960s. She was the first woman to jump above six feet (1.83 m).

Between 1964 and 1980, Irena Kirszenstein-Szewinska of Poland won seven Olympic medals in sprint events

▲ *Soviet athlete Tamara Press won the silver medal in the discus at the 1960 games.*

and the long jump. The Soviets were particularly successful in the throws, behind athletes such as Tamara Press,
Nadezhda Chizhova, and Galina Zybina. Their dominance
would soon be challenged, though.

TITLE IX TAKES HOLD

While Eastern Europeans had been leading women's
track and field for some years, the sport was just starting to become a more widely accepted, mainstream sport
for women in the United States during the early 1970s.
That was largely due to two things. First, the Association for Intercollegiate Athletics for Women (AIAW) was
created in 1971 and began organizing women's college

Pentathlon

Pentathlon is the oldest of the multi-event competitions, dating back to the ancient Greek Olympic
Games. However, the five events that make up a pentathlon have changed throughout the years. In ancient
Greece, the pentathlon included wrestling in addition
to four track-and-field events. Men competed in an
all-track-and-field pentathlon at the Olympic Games
between 1912 and 1924. Women's pentathlon was
in the Games from 1964 to 1980 and included shot
put, high jump, 100-meter hurdles, 200-meter dash,
and long jump. Today, the pentathlon includes fencing,
shooting, swimming, running, and horseback riding.

High Jump

Perhaps no event has evolved as much over time as the high jump. Women's high jump has been included in the Olympic Games since 1928, when women were first allowed to compete in track and field. Early on, athletes jumped as if they were hurdling the bar. Later, many athletes used the Western roll technique, which was a bit like a hurdle over the bar. The modern technique of jumping head first with the back to the ground was popularized by U.S. high jumper Dick Fosbury during the late 1960s. Today, nearly everyone uses the "Fosbury Flop."

Sara Simeoni of Italy was the elite high jumper during the 1970s and early 1980s. She won one gold medal and two silver medals while competing in four Olympic Games between 1972 and 1984. In 1978, she set and then tied a world record at 2.01 meters (6 feet 7 inches).

sports, including track and field. Second, in 1972, Congress passed Title IX. The law stated that any educational institution receiving federal funds had to offer equal athletic opportunities for women.

As more people competed, U.S. women improved on the track. By 1981, the bigger National Collegiate Athletic Association (NCAA) began holding women's national championships, leading to the end of the AIAW.

▲ Title IX led the way for more girls' track-and-field opportunities than ever before.

▲ *Jackie Joyner-Kersee (front center) was a talented hurdler.*

CHAPTER 5

WOMEN BREAK OUT

During the 1970s and early 1980s, the Olympic Games were sometimes overshadowed by politics, terrorism, and **boycotts**. The United States, for example, refused to send a team to the 1980 Games in the former Soviet Union for political reasons. In the Games, the Soviet Union dominated women's track and field. The athletes won 17 medals, including seven gold. Although the Soviet women were very successful in 1980, they would not compete at the next Olympics.

The Soviet Union responded to the U.S. boycott by leading a boycott of the 1984 Games, which took place in Los Angeles. Not having the talented Soviet athletes at the 1984 Games could have been a disaster. Many feared there would not be intense competition, since one of the most talented countries had no athletes at the Games. Instead, it created an opportunity for the U.S. athletes to shine. The first generation of women to largely grow up following the passage of Title IX dominated the track-and-field events. The U.S. women won 16 medals in track and field, including seven gold medals.

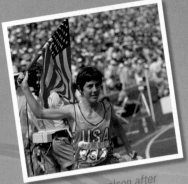

Joan Benoit Samuelson after finishing first in the marathon in the 1984 Olympic Games.

JOAN BENOIT SAMUELSON

Three miles into the first Olympic women's marathon in 1984, Joan Benoit Samuelson took off. Approximately 23 miles (37 km) later, she entered the Los Angeles Coliseum still maintaining that lead. She crossed the finish line as the first Olympic gold medalist in the event. That secured Benoit Samuelson's legacy as one of the best-ever distance runners from the United States. In 2008, at age 50, Benoit Samuelson was still fast enough to qualify and run in the U.S. Olympic trials.

By 1984, any question that women could not handle strenuous activity was officially put to rest. That year, the IOC allowed four of the most grueling events into the program: 400-meter hurdles, 3,000-meter run, marathon, and heptathlon. Those changes helped make the 1984 Games a tremendous success. And several track-and-field icons were born in the process.

JACKIE JOYNER-KERSEE

Growing up with little money and in a bad neighborhood in East St. Louis, Illinois, Jackie Joyner had few opportunities. Then, when she was 10, Title IX was signed into law. For Joyner, who would prove to be perhaps the greatest all-around athlete ever, that law was her opportunity for a better life.

A star basketball player and track-and-field athlete in high school, she earned an athletic **scholarship** to University of California, Los Angeles (UCLA) in 1980. By the 1984 Olympics, she was among the world's best heptathletes and long jumpers.

The 1984 Olympics ended in a near miss for her. She needed to stay within approximately two seconds of her nearest competitor in the final event, the 800-meter run, to win a gold medal. She ended up missing by 2.46 seconds and taking silver. Over the next decade, however, nobody could beat her in a heptathlon.

In 1986, she married one of her coaches, Bob Kersee, becoming Jackie Joyner-Kersee. That same year, she became the first woman to score more than 7,000 points in a heptathlon at the Goodwill Games. With the graceful star from East St. Louis winning back-to-back gold medals in the event, heptathlon was one of the main attractions at the 1988 and 1992 Olympic Games. Joyner-Kersee also won a gold medal in long jump in 1988 and a bronze medal in 1992. In her final Olympics in 1996, she was forced to pull out of the heptathlon due to injury. However, six days later she was back at the long jump pit and earned a bronze medal in the event.

Joyner-Kersee is regarded as one of the greatest athletes ever, male or female. In 2011, the top six scores in heptathlon history belonged to Joyner-Kersee. She once held the long jump world record at 7.49 meters (24 feet 6 4/5 inches). In 2011, that leap stood as the second best of

Goodwill Games

Following the boycotts that watered down the competition at the 1980 and 1984 Olympic Games, U.S. media tycoon Ted Turner created the Goodwill Games to try to bring the United States and Soviet Union closer together. The event featured track and field as well as other events and was held six times between 1986 and 2001.

all time. Multi-event athletes are usually good at a number of events, but they are usually not the best in the world at any one in particular. Joyner-Kersee was the exception. For that, *Sports Illustrated* named her the greatest female athlete of the 20th century.

FLO-JO

Florence Griffith-Joyner married Joyner-Kersee's brother, Al Joyner. Griffith-Joyner, known as Flo-Jo, was the world's elite sprinter during the late 1980s. Flo-Jo made her Olympic debut in 1984 in her hometown of Los Angeles. She finished second in the 200-meter dash. After briefly quitting track and field, Flo-Jo left her ever-lasting mark on the sport in 1988.

At the U.S. Olympic Trials that year, she set a world record in the 100-meter dash at 10.49 seconds. Then, at the Olympic Games in Seoul, South Korea, Flo-Jo won gold medals in the 100- and 200-meter dashes as well as the 4x100 relay. Her 200-meter time of 21.34 seconds was a new world record. She also won a silver medal in the 4x400 relay. With gold medals in the three primary sprinting events—and two world records that still stood in 2011—Flo-Jo is often referred to as the "Fastest Woman in the World."

Flo-Jo retired after the 1988 Olympics at age 28 to pursue other endeavors. She died of heart failure in her home 10 years later. Although Flo-Jo was undeniably fast,

▲ Flo-Jo was also a fashion icon known for her fluorescent-colored outfits on the track and her trademark long, painted fingernails.

At one point, sprinter Gail Devers's feet were so swollen from Graves' Disease, a disorder that affects the thyroid, that doctors considered amputating them. The condition had led to a disappointing performance at the 1988 Olympic Games. As her bouts with fatigue, dizziness, vision loss, and other symptoms continued, Devers lost the ability to walk—and her once promising track-and-field career was seemingly over. But the Southern California native did not accept that fate. After more than two years off, she returned to the 1992 Olympic Games and won the 100-meter dash. Four years later, she won it again and was also part of the winning 4x100 relay.

her life and death were often overshadowed by allegations that she had used illegal performance-enhancing drugs (PEDs). She never did test positive, though.

A GREAT SHAME

After starring as a basketball player at the University of North Carolina, Marion Jones turned her focus to track and field in 1997. With a charming smile and amazing speed, she took the world by storm. At the 2000 Olympic Games in Sydney, Australia, Jones won gold medals in the 100, 200, and 4x400. She also won bronze medals in the long jump and 4x100 relay.

That was the pinnacle of her career, but it would not stay in the record books. In the years following a disappointing, medal-less performance at the 2004 Games, Jones admitted to having taken illegal PEDs. Because of that, all of her medals from the 2000 Games were stripped. That included those of her innocent partners on the relays. Because she had initially lied to U.S. federal investigators about taking PEDs, she also served six months in jail.

Paralympic Games

The Summer Paralympic Games are held every four years, similar to the Olympic Games, and are for athletes with physical and mental disabilities. Held in Beijing, China, a month after the 2008 Olympic Games, the 2008 Paralympic Games showcased 1,041 athletes' talents in track and field, with most events taking place in front of sold-out crowds.

▲ Women race in the 100-meter dash at the 2008 Olympic Games in Beijing.

CHAPTER 6

PLAYING TO WIN

Women's track and field has been growing in participation and acceptance since the women of Vassar College turned up for Field Day in 1895. When the 2000 Olympic Games kicked off in Sydney, Australia, the women's program had the new events of pole vault, hammer throw, and the 20-kilometer walk. The women's program additions continued at the 2008 Games in Beijing, China. With the inclusion of the women's 3,000-meter steeplechase,

Blanka Vlasic

At age 25, Blanka Vlasic won a silver medal in high jump for Croatia at the 2008 Olympic Games. It was her first Olympic medal in three Games. Based on the heights she has cleared, it will probably not be her last. The Croatian high jumper is tied for the second best result of all time for her 2009 jump of 2.08 meters (6 feet 9 4/5 inches). From 2007 to 2010, she won two indoor and two outdoor World Championships titles. Only Germany's Ariane Friedrich came close to Vlasic's top heights during that time.

the men's and women's track-and-field programs were nearly identical.

As women have gained more and more opportunities in track and field, they have continued to achieve at the highest levels and in every event. Although U.S. athletes have gotten a lot of media coverage over the past few decades, athletes from around the world have been thriving in track and field as well. Below are some of the sport's contemporary stars.

STARS IN POLE VAULT

Stacy Dragila became the first star pole-vaulter in the United States. When the women's event debuted at the 1996 U.S. championships, she finished second. No

▲ Pole vault requires all-around athleticism.

American could match Dragila for the next several years. Only Australian superstar Emma George stood in her way. George had set 12 world records in the event between 1995 and 2000.

The stars were set to face off on George's home turf at the 2000 Games in Sydney. However, the anticipated battle was not to be. An injury prevented George from competing at her highest level and from reaching the medal stand. Dragila did not disappoint, though. With a final height of 4.60 meters (15 feet 1 inch) she became the first Olympic gold medalist in women's pole vault.

Dragila was a pioneer in women's pole vault and became the event's first star. But it did not take long for Russia's Yelena Isinbayeva to take over. As of March 2011, she held 23 of the 30 best pole vaults of all time. Among those results were gold medals in the 2004 and 2008 Olympic Games.

TOP MARATHONERS

Women's marathoners have continued to captivate fans ever since Joan Benoit Samuelson won the first Olympic gold medal in 1984. There are many other important marathons besides that of the Olympic Games. Among them are the London Marathon, the New York City Marathon, and the Chicago Marathon. However, the Boston Marathon is considered the most prestigious.

An athlete prepares to throw the shot put.

THROWING FOR GLORY

In most sports, the best results of all time tend to be from more recent times, as athletes continue to develop new and better training techniques. Shot put and discus are an exception. The top throws of all time in those events are from the 1970s and 1980s, when Eastern European countries dominated the events. Hammer throw and javelin have been the opposite, with the best results happening more recently. Either way, all four events have had their share of stars.

Anita Wlodarczyk of Poland set the world record in hammer throw in 2010 at 78.30 meters (256 feet 10 2/3 inches). She was only 24 years old at the time. At the beginning of 2011, it remained the most recent world record set in a major track-and-field event. Nadzeya Ostapchuk of Belarus won the 2010 indoor shot put title as well as the 2008 Olympic bronze medal. Steffi Nerius of Germany has been among the top javelin throwers during the early 2000s. She won a silver medal at the 2004 Olympic Games and a gold medal at the 2009 World Championships. Stephanie Brown Trafton has been a top thrower for the United States. She won the discus gold medal at the 2008 Games.

Dominating Distance

Over the years, African runners have developed into some of the top distance runners in the world. Meseret Defar of Ethiopia proved to be among the world's top 3,000- and 5,000-meter runners. In fact, she won the 3,000 at the Indoor World Championships all four times between 2004 and 2010. In the 5,000, she won the 2004 Olympic gold medal and the 2008 bronze medal. She also won it at the 2007 World Championships.

Possibly more than the other track-and-field events, the women's marathon has seen great women's marathoners from all over the world. Catherine Ndereba of Kenya won the Boston Marathon four times and Olympic silver medals in 2004 and 2008. Through 2010, Great Britain's Paula Radcliffe had the three fastest marathon times ever. Her best was 2:15:25—or two hours, 15 minutes, and 25 seconds—at the 2003 London Marathon. Deena Kastor has been the best American since Benoit Samuelson. She won a bronze medal at the 2004 Olympic Games. She also holds the U.S. record in the marathon with a time of 2:19:36.

New athletes continue to bring new competition to the women's marathon. One of the top Americans is Kara

Goucher. She first became a star running shorter distances on the track. She even ran 5,000- and 10,000-meters at the 2008 Olympic Games. After that, she switched to marathons. It was a good choice—one that would lead to more success. She finished third in her first marathon, the New York City Marathon. Then she finished third in her second try, at the famous Boston Marathon.

SUCCESSFUL SPRINTERS

At the 2008 Games, Jamaican women dominated the short sprints. Shelly-Ann Fraser led a Jamaican sweep in the 100-meter dash. Veronica Campbell-Brown took home her fifth career Olympic medal by winning the 200-meter dash. Teammate Kerron Stewart tied for second in the 100 and finished third in the 200.

Still, the United States has upheld its reputation for strong sprinters. Allyson Felix won silver medals in the 200-meter dash at the 2004 and 2008 Olympic Games. Sanya Richards won a bronze medal in the 400-meter dash at the 2008 Games. She won the event at the 2009 World Championships. Both Felix and Richards helped the United States win a 2008 Olympic gold medal in the 4x400 relay.

As of 2011, one of the United States' biggest stars in the sprints is Carmelita Jeter. The Southern California native has established herself as one of the country's top 100-meter runners. Although she failed to qualify for the

▲ *Kara Goucher (left) runs with the front of the pack during the 2009 Boston Marathon.*

2008 Games, she won bronze medals in the 100 at the 2007 and 2009 World Championships. When she clocked 10.64 seconds at a 2009 meet in China, she became the second fastest woman of all time. Only Florence Griffith-Joyner had run faster times.

Steeplechase

The 3,000-meter steeplechase is a relatively new event in women's track and field. Modeled after horse racing, steeplechase involves running around a track and jumping hurdles. Some of the hurdles have a water pit after them. The water pits are obstacles the athletes must power through. In total, the athletes jump 28 hurdles, seven of which have water pits. When the event debuted at the Olympics in 2008, Gulnara Galkina-Samitova of Russia won in a world-record time of 8:58.81.

BRIGHT FUTURE

Female track-and-field athletes have been fighting the odds since the beginning of the sport. To each challenge, however, the athletes have responded. They have proven that they are not only capable of competing in every track-and-field event, but that they can achieve great things. With nothing to hold the next generation of women back, the possibilities are limitless.

▲ Competitors in the steeplechase try to continue their speed and running form through the water pits.

GLOSSARY

board: The area of a runway from which a long jumper or triple jumper must jump. Stepping beyond the board results in a foul.

boycotts: Protests in which one group refuses to participate in relations with another group, often due to political reasons. In sports, countries sometimes boycott events held in other countries.

cross train: To train for one sport or event by doing exercises not directly related to the event. For example, a runner might cross train by riding a bike.

foul: A violation of regulations in a field event or an action against another runner in a race deemed to have hindered that runner's race.

hurdles: A sprint race in which obstacles are set up on the track. The goal is to clear the obstacles, or hurdles, without losing speed.

intermediate: The middle stage. Youth athletes run the 300-meter intermediate hurdles rather than the 400-meter hurdles of higher levels.

laps: Full journeys around the track or racecourse. Each full journey is called a lap.

medley: A relay race in which a team works together to run the total distance. Runners do not all run the same distance.

meet: A track-and-field competition.

momentum: The force gained by an object moving.

pacing: Saving energy while completing a task so that a strong effort can be maintained the entire time.

ring: The circle throwers stand in while executing a throw.

scholarship: Money given to a student to help them pay for classes or other college expenses as a reward for skills in a specific area, such as athletics.

stamina: Strength to endure fatigue or hardship.

starting blocks: Footholds that sprinters use to start a race. They allow runners to push off and begin a race at a faster speed.

torso: The trunk of the body.

FOR MORE INFORMATION

BOOKS

Aaseng, Nathan. *Track and Field*. San Diego, CA: Lucent, 2002.
This book contains a brief history of track and field.

Housewright, Ed. *Winning Track and Field for Girls*. New York: Mountain Lion, 2004.
This book introduces readers to every women's track-and-field event. It gives specific training plans and other tips for each event while also highlighting some of the stars in each event.

Joyner-Kersee, Jackie. *A Kind of Grace: The Autobiography of the World's Greatest Female Athlete*. New York: Warner, 1997.
The autobiography of U.S. Olympic heptathlon champion Jackie Joyner-Kersee, who many believe to be one of the greatest athletes of all time.

Smith, Lissa, ed. *Nike Is a Goddess: The History of WOMEN in Sports*. New York: Atlantic Monthly, 1998.
This book tells the story of women in various sports, including track and field, softball, figure skating, swimming, soccer, hockey, basketball, and others.

WEBSITES

International Association of Athletics Federations
www.iaaf.org
The official website of IAAF, which governs world track and field. It contains information about top athletes and events around the world.

Track & Field News
www.trackandfieldnews.com
This website contains up-to-date news about track and field from around the world. It is the website for the popular magazine, *Track & Field News.*

United States Olympic Committee
www.teamusa.org
The official website of the United States Olympic Committee contains news and features about the top U.S. Olympians and Olympic hopefuls.

USA Track & Field
www.usatf.org
The official website of USA Track & Field, the national governing body for the sport in the United States, this site includes news, events, stats, bios of elite athletes, and more information about all levels of track and field in the country.

INDEX

PLACES TO VISIT

Hayward Field

1580 East 15th Avenue, Eugene, OR 97403
(541) 346-4461
www.goducks.com/ViewArticle.dbml?DB_OEM_
ID=500&ATCLID=22187
The home of the University of Oregon track-and-field teams is
one of the most famous track-and-field facilities in the country.

U.S. Olympic Training Center

One Olympic Plaza, Colorado Springs, CO 80909
(888) 659-8687 or (719) 866-4618
www.teamusa.org
The Olympic Training Center offers free public tours that include
a video and a walking tour of the complex, showcasing the
training facilities of many U.S. Olympic and Paralympic hopefuls.

ABOUT THE AUTHOR

Chrös McDougall is a sportswriter and author
who specializes in Olympic sports. A former
400-meter runner in high school, McDougall
later covered gymnastics at the 2008 Olympic
Games and writes for TeamUSA.org, the U.S.
Olympic Committee's website. He lives in the
Twin Cities of Minnesota with his wife.

ABOUT THE CONTENT CONSULTANT

Elliott Denman is a New Jersey-based writer
who focuses on track and field and other
Olympic sports. A member of the 1956 U.S.
Olympic track and field team—he placed 11th
in the 50-kilometer racewalk—he went on to an
award-winning career in sports journalism and
has covered 12 Olympic Games.